COPYCAT

For Marsha Dixon

A Red Fox Book

Published by Random House Children's Books
20 Vauxhall Bridge Road, London SW1V 2SA

A division of Random House UK Ltd.
London Melbourne Sydney Auckland
Johannesburg and agencies throughout the world

Copyright © 1994 by Ruth Brown

1 3 5 7 9 10 8 6 4 2

First published by Andersen Press Ltd 1994

Red Fox edition 1996

Printed in Hong Kong

RANDOM HOUSE UK Limited Reg. No. 954009

ISBN 0 09 960411 6

COPYCAT
RUTH BROWN

Red Fox

There was once a black cat called Holly. She was the mother of Baby and Buddy and they all lived with Bessie the dog. Baby was shy and kept to herself but Buddy was the opposite. Buddy was a copycat.

Holly liked to daydream by
the window – so did Buddy.

Baby liked to sleep on the
window seat – so did Buddy.

When Holly sat by the fire
warming her back, Buddy
warmed his feet, unless

He even copied the squirrels,

and the birds,

Bessie was
chewing a bone and Buddy
decided that what was right for
Bessie was right for Copycat.

But Buddy was wrong.

Cats' teeth aren't made for
chewing bones, and,

Even though his tongue
hangs out now, Buddy
hasn't changed a bit.

He's still the same
old Copycat.

Some
bestselling Red Fox
picture books